SHELTER FROM THE WIND

MARION DANE BAUER

MARSHALL CAVENDISH CHILDREN

Marshall Cavendish *Classics*

Marshall Cavendish is bringing classic titles from children's
literature back into print for a new generation. We have selected
titles that have withstood the test of time, and we welcome any
suggestions for future titles in this program.
To learn more, visit our Web site: www.marshallcavendish.us/kids.

Marshall Cavendish Corporation
99 White Plains Road
Tarrytown, NY 10591
www.marshallcavendish.us/kids

Library of Congress Cataloging-in-Publication Data
Bauer, Marion Dane.
Shelter from the wind / by Marion Dane Bauer. — 1st Marshall Cavendish
classics ed.
p. cm.
Summary: When twelve-year-old Stacy gets fed up with her pregnant
stepmother and leaves her Oklahoma panhandle home, she is led by a pair
of dogs, one about to whelp, to the home of Old Ella, who gives her a new
perspective on life.
ISBN 978-0-7614-5687-2
[1. Runaways—Fiction. 2. Dogs—Fiction. 3. Oklahoma—Fiction.] I. Title.
PZ7.B3262Sh 2010
[Fic]—dc22
2009014677

Book design by Becky Terhune

Printed in China (E)
1 3 5 6 4 2

mc Marshall Cavendish

In memory of Peter,
who owned the real Nimue

ONE

STACY SLAMMED THE DOOR BEHIND HER. THE JUNE heat rose in her face, along with the Oklahoma dust. She rubbed the grit from her eyes angrily and rammed her cowboy hat down on her head so the wind couldn't catch it. Then she clattered down the wooden steps which led from her apartment, the apartment she and Daddy had had to themselves before Barbara came, and went down the side of Daddy's grocery store to the alley. At the bottom she kicked a rusty can.

Damn Barbara! Stacy wished she had said it inside. "Damn you, Barbara!" Only her father wouldn't have liked it. Barbara was his wife. Barbara was going to have his baby. Barbara had grown big and fat with a belly that stuck out almost to her knees when she sat down, and she whined about the heat and the dust and about her back hurting. Stacy picked up a rock and clanged it against a garbage can. Then she started walking,

1

kicking up puffs of dust as she moved down the alley lined with garbage cans and old boards and tar paper and hunks of rusty metal.

For five years, ever since Stacy had been six, she and Daddy had managed by themselves. More than managed, they had been happy. Daddy did the cooking and took care of their four-room apartment and his store. After school and in the summer Stacy would sit on the stool at the window in the front of the cool, dark little store that always smelled of raw meat and bread and scrubbed wooden floors. She would read and talk to Daddy when he wasn't busy with customers and even manage the cash register part of the time.

After Barbara came last year she did all the cooking. She couldn't cook as well as Daddy. She sat on the stool in the front of the store, too. Stacy knew Daddy would be sorry about Barbara when he realized that his daughter was gone.

She hadn't known when she left the apartment what she was going to do. Barbara had been yelling again, her voice shrill and cross, and Daddy had been sitting there, staring into his empty coffee cup, and Stacy had just gone through the door with a bang. She hadn't known until she was starting down the alley that she was really going to go this time. She had been thinking about it for a long time, planning where she would go and what she would take, but now she was started, and she didn't have anything, not even a plan.

The wind pushed against her. It blew warm now at 8:30 in the morning. Soon it would blow hot across the high plains. Stacy put her hands into the pockets of her jeans and walked with her head bent watching the dusty tips of her sneakers. When she got to the street, she turned left and walked the half a block to the highway and then turned right on the highway and began walking away from her home and her father's store. She could hear the rusty Seven-Up sign that creaked rhythmically in the doorway, the sound she had gone to sleep to as long as she could remember, but she didn't turn around to look.

She kept walking away, the way her mother had once before when Stacy was very small, only her mother had gone in a car. At least that was what Stacy had heard people whisper in her father's store. Her mother had gone in a car with a man, and she hadn't come back. Stacy had come home from first grade to find her father cutting meat with his face all fierce and dark, but he wouldn't say anything except, "She's gone," when Stacy had asked for her mother. If Stacy cried at night, he would come and lift her out of her bed in his big arms with the sprouts of black hair on them, and he would rock her in Mother's rocking chair that creaked like the Seven-Up sign. He never sang the way her mother used to, and he didn't talk to her even, but he held her, and he rocked. Stacy would feel the warm firmness of his chest and the tight way his arms held her and stop crying. But that had all been a long time ago—long before Barbara.

In the yellow-brown shadow of the grain elevator, Stacy stopped and looked up for the first time. The road and the prairie stretched out in front of her like a table, unwavering. A walker might step off that distant edge into the sky. There was more sky in Oklahoma than anything else. "The bluest sky in the world," Daddy always said, and Daddy had been a sailor once and had seen the world, or a lot of it—but he had come back here. Stacy wasn't going to come back.

She squinted at the sky, looking for the mesas which stood up like black shelves against the horizon. She couldn't see them, but she knew she would come to them if she only walked west far enough. That was where she would go, to the mesas first, the tableland the Spanish had named, then finally maybe to the Rocky Mountains.

Her mother used to talk about the Rocky Mountains, about streams, clear and cold even in the middle of summer, about peaks where the snow never melted, about black-green pines and scrub oak and graceful aspen with leaves that trembled in every breeze. There you could find shelter from the wind that never stopped blowing through the Oklahoma panhandle. Stacy could remember her mother, restless with the constant wind, fretting and wiping at the dust it laid on everything in the store and the apartment. Stacy had always liked the wind that whipped her hair and pulled at her clothes, but she would like the Rockies better. Her mother did.

Still not looking back at Cimarron City where she had always lived, she started off at an angle across the yellow stubble of a wheat field, walking away from the sun.

TWO

THE SUN WAS RELENTLESS. STACY NO LONGER KNEW what time it was, but the heat shimmered off the ground in waves. She had left the wheat land behind and the plains rolled in front of her like a ragged brown sea. She sat down on an outcropping of wind-carved sandstone on the crest of one of the prairie waves and turned up her jeans to examine her scratched legs. She had torn her shirt on a barbed wire fence. She wished she had put her boots on this morning instead of her sneakers. She hadn't been prepared for anything. She hadn't brought any money or a change of clothes or even food or water. Especially water. She, who had always been an Okie, had never known anything except this dry hostile land, knew the importance of water on the prairie, and she had walked out of town like a dude who knew nothing. Without even water! She took off her hat and wiped the sweat off her forehead. The wind ruffled her damp brown hair. She tossed it aside and wished once more that it were cut short . . . boy short. Only her father wouldn't hear of it.

What he didn't understand was that she hated girl things, all girl things. She wanted to be a boy. She hated her developing breasts that made embarrassing bumps in her tee shirts, and she often wore her father's old shirts buttoned up to her throat and with the sleeves cut short so no one could tell. Lisa's chest was still as flat as a boy's, and Lisa envied Stacy her changing body. Stacy didn't tell even Lisa how much she hated it. But she hooked her thumbs in the pockets of her jeans like the boys did and she studied the way the older guys walked and imitated it. She could even swear like she heard guys swear, but not in front of her dad and Barbara. They wanted her to be a *lady*, whatever that was. Being a lady didn't include wearing jeans or knowing how to swear.

Stacy looked back toward town. She could still see the towering block which was the grain elevator, small now in the distance, but nothing else. The grain elevator could be seen for many miles. Walking out of sight of that would take a long time. She sighed. She had botched it, but she wasn't going to go back. She had been gone too long already. If she went back she would have to explain, to Barbara and to her father with Barbara listening. She couldn't do that. And if she went back she wouldn't be able to leave again, ever, because they would be expecting it. Somehow the whole point of running away was that they would never expect it.

She got up and began walking again, watching more carefully for the cactus and yucca, the purple-flowered thistle and last year's tumbleweed. It seemed as though everything that grew on the high plains had some kind of sharpness to protect itself. Everything except Stacy. Her foot brushed against some prickly pear, and she grimaced.

Stacy's head was light with the heat, her eyes gritty and burning, her tongue thick when she crested a hill and dropped down a gully where a lone cottonwood tree rustled in the wind. Near the base of the tree, water seeped out from under some rocks and disappeared into the surrounding ground without a trace. Except for the tree. The tree was there because of the water.

Stacy knelt on the ground and scooped a small hollow at the base of the dampened rocks. Slowly it filled with water, and she bent over to drink, feeling the sand between her teeth. Finally, her thirst still unsatisfied but no longer an agony, she crawled into the shade of the cottonwood and, looking around briefly to check for snakes, she lay down with her head pillowed on her arm and was almost immediately asleep.

The western sky was coloring when she woke up, startled by an approaching roar. Hardly having time to recollect where she was, she gathered herself into a ball at the base of the tree and looked through the leaves at a small plane which passed over her close and then circled to pass again. That was Mr. Shannon's plane. He was probably out looking for her.

Mr. Shannon was a rancher. He had survived the dust bowl years in the 1930s, the dirty thirties people here called them, and now owned one of the largest ranches in the area; but he always seemed to Stacy to be withered and dry, as though he had never gotten enough water in all the years of prosperity. When he came into her dad's store and Stacy was there, he would always wordlessly hand her a candy bar for herself to add to his order. There was something, though, about the way he looked at her that made the candy taste flat and dry. She held her knees tightly and made herself small in the shade of the tree. The plane had rumbled out of sight before she realized again how thirsty and hungry she was.

Stacy sat watching the sky turn a pale gray, then charcoal. The horizon was a black line—infinitely distant. She shivered. All of the warmth seemed to leave the air in this high panhandle country the moment the sun set. She tried again to get some water and then curled up, pressing herself against the ground for warmth. Her tongue filled her mouth again. She wondered how long it took to die of thirst. She wondered if they would find her body before the buzzards came.

The stars were shining pinpricks in a black enamel cup. There was no moon, and the stars gave only the illusion of light. The wind soughed. The leaves of the cottonwood tree rattled and whispered constantly. There was no other sound. She could have been alone in the world except for the stars and the wind and the tree. She thought about her comfortable bed at the front of their apartment, about hearing her father's and Barbara's voices, quiet from the kitchen, about the purr of a car going by. Even the wind sounded different from her bed. It squeaked her dad's Seven-Up sign and rattled garbage cans up and down the alley and made the screen door on Joe's Bar and Grill across the street bang like a firecracker, but they were all familiar sounds. Out here the wind cried like a lonely child, but Stacy didn't cry. She lay still and listened. She felt naked, exposed, as though night eyes watched her and only she could not see.

Stacy awakened in the darkness to feel breath on her neck. Some shape loomed over her, sniffing. It was like a dream where you are running but are held fast to the ground and your cries of terror are soundless. Stacy closed her eyes tightly. In a moment she would wake up. Something cold and wet touched her cheek, and she screamed. She sat up with a jerk, the trunk of the tree behind her, and her cries raced over the prairie without finding even an answering echo. She screamed and screamed, but the creature, whatever it had been, had bounded away with her first cry. Hugging her knees and trembling violently, she pressed her back against the trunk of the old cottonwood. She stared into the night. There was nothing to see and only the wind to hear.

She didn't sleep again. She sat without moving, her eyes and ears straining. Occasionally she would glance back quickly over one shoulder or the other, though she couldn't see any farther behind than she could in front of her. What kind of animal had it been? A bobcat? There were still bobcats in the country. A mountain lion? One of Mr. Shannon's men had shot a mountain lion only last year, but there weren't often mountain lions any more. Stacy shuddered and tried to look up into the branches of the tree nonetheless. A coyote? But why would it have come right up to her that way? No animal Stacy knew would come that close to a human, even one asleep. A rattler? Snakes don't snuffle, and they don't feel wet. Stacy wished she had stayed at home. When it was light she would go back, which wouldn't be difficult, even as far from the highway as she was. She had only to walk back to the grain elevator. After all, why should she let Barbara run her out of her own home? It was her home, hers more than it was Barbara's.

Not until the sky was beginning to lighten to a slate gray again could Stacy make out the figure that sat about fifty feet on the other side of the spring. It looked like a wolf. She gasped and started to rise. Then another figure, larger than the first, moved into place, and Stacy stood without moving, holding onto the trunk of the tree. Wolves? She didn't know when anyone had last seen wolves in this country. Her heart was beating frantically and her breath came in sharp gasps that cut her chest like a knife. Wolves didn't bother people either, unless they were starved. There were plenty of rabbits about, and prairie dogs and pocket gophers and raccoons. No reason for wolves to be hungry.

If she ran, she would make herself more of a target. Stacy knew that. But it wasn't so much her knowledge of what she should do as the weakness of her knees that kept her standing there, confronting the silent figures. They sat as still as if they had been carved from stone. As Stacy stood, holding onto the protection of her tree, the sky grew paler. She could make out the sharp points of their ears, the bulk of their bodies.

"Shoo!" she said, in a tiny voice that wouldn't have scared a kitten. "Shoo! Go away!"

One of the animals rose with a slow dignity and stalked toward her.

"Please," she said, her voice only a whisper now. "Go away. I'm going to go back home. Don't hurt me." She gripped the tree to keep from collapsing. The animal paused at the rocks and lapped at the scooped-out hollow Stacy had left. Stacy saw herself running, climbing the tree, throwing a rock, but she could not move. Slowly still, the huge figure raised its head and then walked the last few feet that separated them. Stacy felt a cool, moist nose against her hand, and even as she stifled her scream, she saw. It was a dog. A large, white dog. She slid to the ground and put her arms around the animal's soft neck and cried and laughed against its shoulder. The dog licked her face.

THREE

THE SKY FLAMED WITH THE APPROACH OF MORNING. Stacy sat and stroked the gentle white dog, rubbed her ears until she groaned with pleasure, scratched her neck and chest. She was a beautiful German shepherd, pure white except for the slightest tinge of beige down her back, who watched Stacy with affectionate amber eyes and licked her face frequently. Her partner, a large male, also a white shepherd, remained aloof a short distance away. He watched Stacy and his mate closely but without tension or fear. He sat with his head high, his ears stiffly erect, and waited.

Stacy ran her hands down the dog's sides. Her coat was sleek and well cared for. Her belly swelled. She was obviously no wild dog.

"Where do you live?" she asked, and the gentle animal licked her face again. "I'd sure like some of whatever you've been eating to make you so fat," Stacy added. Her fear past, she began to realize again how hungry and thirsty she was. She knelt at the rocks in front of her and tried to sip at the muddy water. When she looked up, the female had joined her mate, but stood quietly, already turned away, but looking back at Stacy.

Stacy stood up. "Oh, don't leave me!" she said. She suddenly knew she would be alone if these dogs disappeared, more alone than she had been before they came. Neither dog moved. Stacy hurried toward them. The male shifted his weight from one paw to the other. He didn't look menacing, but when Stacy reached out to touch him he backed away, stopping barely out of her reach.

"Don't you like me?" she asked. He cocked his head, his tongue lolling out of the side of his mouth, but he made no move in either direction. The female came up to Stacy and put her muzzle under Stacy's hand and nudged her.

Stacy followed the dogs away from the just-rising sun. She had forgotten now about going back home. They crossed the dry bed of a stream, probably the Cimarron River. Stacy hesitated on the edge and then followed the dogs' exact footprints carefully. She knew that these streams, running underground most of the year, could be treacherous. Ground that looked firm could suddenly sink under a person's feet. She followed the dogs up the other side of the streambed where they paused to lap at a pool of water which had risen to the surface. On another day, Stacy knew, that surface water might be a hundred yards away or nowhere at all. She tried to walk out to the pool, but the ground began slipping under her feet and she backed away quickly. With envy she watched the dogs drink, though the water was murky.

Stacy didn't know where she was going. She had ceased to think about it as she followed the two white animals who adjusted their easy lope for her slower and more awkward walking. The male kept about six feet ahead of her. The female circled back frequently, pushed at Stacy's hand with her muzzle, then turned to follow her mate. Stacy was sure they were leading her somewhere. The land rose and fell. Clumps of flowers appeared, purple and yellow and white, in every depression that might hold the runoff from a rain. Sunflowers lined a dirt road she crossed. She hesitated in the middle of the road. It would be easier walking than the grassland, but any rancher she met would be sure to ask questions. Besides, the dogs didn't slow down. The tough buffalo grass which clung to the dusty surface of the prairie made each step uneven. She passed a utility pole and heard its electric hum, as steady as the wind. The dogs never stopped. Grasshoppers scattered before her with every step.

Reaching the top of a rise, she could see Black Mesa, a dark line in the distance, and other smaller mesas and buttes sprang up before her. Stacy stopped once to look back and realized that she could no longer see the grain elevator. She thought the land swells must be in the way. She couldn't have come that far. She was surprised at how frightened she felt to be cut off from that ugly object in the shadow of which she had always lived. She turned back to follow the dogs. She mustn't lose sight of the dogs.

The prairie grew more rugged and the walking more difficult. Even the dogs stopped frequently, their tongues dripping. The female waited for Stacy, the male only for his mate. Stacy was beginning to feel light-headed, past hunger or thirst, too fatigued to move but afraid of losing the dogs if she stopped. The sun reflected off the ground, pressed down on her shoulders. The wind moaned.

She had been walking almost in a trance for some time when she and the two dogs crested a hill and looked down into a bowl of land in the center of which was a small, red sandstone house with a tent-shaped roof, its door open. Stacy sat down abruptly, sat and looked at the crude little stone house. She was still sitting when the two dogs came out of the house, cavorting around a miniature old woman whose face was hidden deep inside the kind of cotton sunbonnet pioneer women used to wear. The stiff figure stomped up the hill toward Stacy without hesitation. She used a cane, but it seemed to stomp, too.

The woman poked Stacy with her cane. "Who're you?"

"Stacy," she answered, drawing a breath. She wasn't going to cry. She never cried. When she was little she cried over her mother, but not any more. She never cried over Barbara.

"How'd you get here?" the woman asked, with another poke of her cane. Her hand on the cane was brown, the knuckles enlarged and blue-purple veins knotting across the back.

"I walked," Stacy answered. Stacy hadn't tried to look at the face inside the shadow of the sunbonnet, but it wasn't the kind of voice that gave any choice about answering. She looked down at a pair of engineer's boots, firmly laced.

"Walked? Why you're five miles from the highway."

"No, ma'am. I didn't come from the highway. I came from Cimarron City."

"Hmmmmmph," the woman grunted, as though it was worse to have come from Cimarron City than from the highway. "That's all of fifteen miles. Have you got a head on you, girl?"

"I ran away," Stacy replied, as though that were some kind of answer.

"Might have figured. Nimue," she said, turning to the white female who had been sitting close beside her, "don't we have enough to do with your time coming without you dragging home a stray. More trouble, that's all it is. More trouble and another mouth. Well, come on. You look like you could use some tending." The woman turned away and began walking toward her small house.

"I can't," Stacy said. "I can't go any farther." The woman didn't turn back. "If you had the gumption to run all this way from Cimarron City, you can walk a few more steps to my house. I'm not going to carry you." And she proceeded down the slope without pausing to see whether Stacy would follow. After the woman had disappeared back into the hut, Stacy stood up and made her way down the hill.

Standing in the doorway of the hut, Stacy blinked to adjust her eyes to the darkness. For a moment she could see nothing, and the old woman seemed to have disappeared.

"Come over here," a voice said, commanding. Stacy stepped inside and as her eyes grew accustomed to the dim light she made out the woman off to her right pouring something, pouring water from a tin pitcher into an enameled basin. She walked toward the woman as though compelled. The woman motioned to a wooden chair. It had been painted white once, but much of the paint was worn off now. The table she sat down to was the same. Stacy leaned over the basin and bathed her face, cupping the water in her hands and feeling it against her eyes and in the edges of her hair. Then she cupped her hands and began to drink.

"Here!" The woman took the basin away and Stacy thought for an instant she was going to slap her hands. "We don't waste water around here, but we don't have to drink what we wash with." She pushed the basin back toward Stacy and handed her a cake of hard yellow soap. "Wash," she ordered. "You'll feel better. Probably look better, too. I'll get some fresh water for drinking." She clumped to the door with a bucket in her hand. Framed in the open door, the harsh light from outside silhouetting her, she turned back and said, "If you were going to run away, didn't you even have the sense to carry water?"

Stacy shook her head miserably.

The old woman looked down at the two dogs, who were lying on each side of the door, panting. "If you had to round me up a stray, couldn't you have found one with a brain or two? Well," she grunted, turning to go out, "I guess nobody with too much sense would be out here."

After Stacy had washed her face and hands, she looked around. The open cabin was roughly divided into rooms by the placement of the furniture. A large brass bed with a patchwork quilt on it was in one corner. Across from it was a faded couch which sagged in the middle. On the side where Stacy sat at the table was an old cook stove, the kind that burned wood, and a cupboard. Stacy was wondering if there was any food in the cupboard when the woman returned, setting the bucket of water in the corner and pointing to the line on Stacy's arms where the washing had been discontinued.

"Take off your things and wash all over. I'll find something to cover you, and after you've eaten you can wash those dirty clothes."

The woman went into the area by the bed, reached behind a red curtain strung on a rope across one corner, and brought out a faded cotton dress similar to the one she was wearing. She also took off her deep sunbonnet and stuck it on a hook behind the curtain. Her hair was a grizzled gray and, drawn back with a red string at her neck, hung almost to her waist. Stacy turned away and began slowly to remove her clothes. The cool water had felt good at first, but now she wished she were lying in a nice hot tub at home.

Stacy washed to the woman's satisfaction and put on the dress, which hung loosely to her ankles. She sat down at the table and looked at her hostess. Her skin was brown and deeply creased. She reminded Stacy of those doll faces carved from apples and left to dry. Only her eyes, blue as the Oklahoma sky, didn't fit with the apple face.

"Well," the woman said, stopping halfway between the stove and the table with a bowl in her hand, "do you always sit down to eat with the wash water in the middle of the table?"

"Oh!" Stacy jumped up guiltily. She picked up the bowl and then looked around. Of course there was no sink. The woman had gone outside for the water. "What do I do with it?" she asked after a moment.

"You can drink it, if you're still of a mind to, but if I was you I'd throw it out on the flowers. You're not the only being who would relish some water."

Stacy stepped to the door with the basin in her hands and blinked in the sunshine. Flowers? she wondered, looking out at the sagebrush and buffalo grass. Then she looked down and saw a row of red petunias, hugging the narrow strip of shade beside the stone house. She walked along carefully pouring the water on the row.

When she came back in, the woman had poured a glass of water for her. There was a bowl of cold bean soup and cold corn bread, too.

"Drink it slowly," she advised, when Stacy picked up the glass eagerly, "and not too much at a time or you'll get sick. I wanted you to cool off some before you began to drink."

Stacy let the water run over her tongue. A drink had never tasted so good. The cold soup and corn bread, without butter or jelly, were good, too.

"I only use the stove at night when it's summer," the woman explained. "Chopping wood is hard work, especially the cedar and juniper that burn right."

Stacy looked over at the stove. She had seen pictures of stoves like that, but she had never seen a real one. At home they had a gas stove, and the blue ring of flame appeared instantly at the twist of a knob. Barbara complained about the heat of cooking during the summer, though the air conditioner roared in the window just over the sink.

Stacy looked up. A wooden beam ran the length of the house, from next to the door to next to the stove. It was really all that separated the two "rooms." The entire length of the beam was carefully painted in tiny red and white checks.

"Who did that?" Stacy asked, pointing.

The woman looked up at the beam and her creases deepened into a smile. "My husband, Ben, came out here in '28. This was about the last place in the country a man could still homestead, though there wasn't much left even here. He got this 160 acres, though, and some state land to lease." She stopped as though she had answered Stacy's question.

"Did Ben build the house?" Stacy asked, to get her started again.

The woman nodded. "Ben wouldn't have a dugout for his wife the way lots of folks did. An old Mexican showed him how to cut the sandstone out of the mesas, and they worked together for about six months, cutting the stone and hauling it and hauling the wood for the floors and beams and the cedar shingles from Clayton. That's over in New Mexico." Again she stopped.

"And the beam. Ben painted the beam?" Stacy persisted.

The old woman looked at the beam, and her face softened. Her eyes seemed to take on a new light. "When they had the house finished, winter had set in, and well, I guess it was a long winter." Stacy turned to look again at the checks that held the woman's gaze. A long winter indeed! "Ben had farmed in Arkansas, but that was his Daddy's farm, and mostly there you can look out and see your near neighbor. He'd never had a winter all to himself. I didn't come out here until summer. Took the train from Arkansas all the way to

Clayton. The preacher in Clayton married us in his parlor, then we came here in the spring wagon. Took two days, even being pulled by a good team. It's fifty miles, I guess."

Silence again inside the cabin, and Stacy could hear the wind wailing at the windows as though it wanted to come in. Then the voice continued. "Ben said he would have liked to paint flowers and things, the things I was leaving behind in Arkansas, but he wasn't any good at pictures, so he just made checks, like Mamma's tablecloth at home, a few squares a day. Said it kept him from going loco and just starting out across the prairie. I guess people do that sometimes." The woman looked hard at Stacy, and she squirmed a little inside the dress.

"Maybe I should have tried painting a checker-board," Stacy said, grimly.

The woman's eyes snapped, but the creases around them deepened. "Maybe you should have," she said.

FOUR

"YOUR NAME IS STACY?" THE WOMAN ASKED.

Stacy nodded.

"Mine is Ella. Folks around here call me Old Ella."

Stacy nodded again. The two of them sat in silence, Stacy waiting for Old Ella to ask questions, but she didn't ask anything. After a few moments Stacy began to feel uncomfortable, then annoyed. Didn't this funny old lady even care that she had run away from home? Didn't she want to find out who she was and where she had come from and why she had run away? Stacy began to fidget.

"I hate my stepmother," she blurted out finally.

Old Ella, who had been examining her gnarled hands, looked up slowly. "That must feel pretty bad," she said.

The response wasn't what Stacy had expected. "What?" she asked.

"Hating. Your stepmother. Especially if you live with her every day."

"Yes, ma'am. I do. For a year now. She married my father."

"Mmmm, stands to reason," Ella said, "if she's your stepmother."

Stacy flushed. Did she sound stupid? "I'm going to find my mother, my real mother." Was that what she was going to do? Stacy hadn't known until she heard herself say it.

"Where's she?" Ella got up and picked up the dishes and carried them to the cold stove. She left her cane over the back of her chair.

"I...I'm not sure. She grew up in the Rockies, the mountains, you know. She always loved them. I think when she left she would have gone back there. I'm sure Daddy knows where she is—because they got a divorce and all—but he never would tell me."

"So you're going to walk to the Rockies?"

Stacy felt herself coloring again. The idea did sound dumb, stated so plainly, but what else was there to do? "Yes," she said, more boldly than she felt. Old Ella wouldn't let her go farther, surely. She would call somebody and send Stacy home, though of course there was no telephone here. But there must be some way. No adult would help a kid run away.

"You'd better get yourself some water before you go," was all Ella said.

Stacy stood up. The woman's dress hung loosely all about her. It felt strange. Wouldn't Barbara laugh if she could see her now. Barbara was perpetually wanting Stacy to wear a dress. "I've always wanted a daughter, and look at that," Barbara would say, sighing at Stacy's jeans and her dad's old shirts. "I'm not your daughter anyway," Stacy would answer fiercely, and then Barbara would get that tight look around her mouth and turn away.

"I have your dress on," Stacy said. "I can't go in this."

Ella looked up from the dishes she was washing with a rag and a little water in the enameled basin. "So you do," she said. "Well, it won't take you long to get your things washed and dried. Come. I'll show you."

Taking up the bucket and the cake of yellow soap, Ella handed them to Stacy, then she pointed from the doorway. "The spring and the pot for heating water and the washtub's around back. There's some cedar for your fire. Gather some brush to get it started."

Stacy stepped out into the blinding sun.

"Oh," Ella added, "here are matches." She handed Stacy a box of wooden matches from her pocket. "Don't waste them," she said, disappearing back into the cool darkness of the house.

Stacy headed toward the back of the house in the direction Ella had pointed, grumbling. She was surprised Ella hadn't expected her to rub two sticks together.

At the back corner of the house, Stacy stopped and caught her breath. In front of her was a low, spreading tree, its branches, which reached almost to the ground on every side, heavy with fragile, brushlike pink blossoms. There were few trees in Cimarron City and those that were there were mostly cotton-woods. Trees required water and care. She set down the bucket and the bar of soap and walked up to the tree slowly, as though it might get startled and run away if she weren't careful. She touched one of the feathery blossoms with one finger, and then slowly she walked around the tree. She had never seen anything more beautiful. She positively ached with delight. After she had circled the tree twice, she walked back to the door, still in a trance. She stood in the doorway a moment, waiting for her eyes to adjust to the darkness. Ella was sitting on the couch with some mending in her lap. She was looking at Stacy with a waiting expression.

"The tree," Stacy said, "that beautiful tree! What is it?"

"That's my wedding tree."

"Your wedding tree?"

Ella nodded and smiled at her mending.

Stacy swallowed her impatience. She wished Old Ella would tell her a few things without her asking a hundred questions. You'd think she'd be glad of someone to talk to, she thought.

"Why is it called a wedding tree?"

"It's a mimosa, really." Ella still didn't look up.

Stacy sat down in the doorway, tucking Ella's dress around her feet, and waited.

Ella continued, still concentrating on her mending, a small recitation, a story she had told—to whom? herself?—many times. "Ben brought it all the way from Arkansas and planted it there when he first came to homestead. All wrapped in paper he carried it, gently as if it was a baby, with good, black Arkansas dirt packed around its roots. It was just this time of June when he brought me out here, and the tree was little, barely more than a twig, but it was blooming."

"So it was your wedding tree," Stacy said, looking at the deep creases and the crisscross of fine lines in Ella's face and trying to imagine her as a young bride.

Ella looked up and smiled again, but the smile was aimed at some point in the air past Stacy's shoulder. "In the evening, when the work was done, I used to sit out there and watch that tree. It kept me from crying to go back to my people."

Stacy stood up. Everybody was always wanting to go back somewhere. This was Stacy's home, had always been. But she would find her mother. She knew she could find her if she looked hard enough. She went outside to look for the spring.

At home Barbara did the wash in the automatic machines at the laundromat. Daddy had done it before Barbara came. Stacy had never had to wash her own clothes. By the time she had drawn buckets of water from the spring to fill the black kettle on legs, the buckets pulling at her arm and banging against her leg as she carried them, and had gathered brush and lit the fire under the kettle, she was exhausted, and she hadn't even started to wash yet.

When the water was hot, she dipped it into a round, tin washtub and rubbed her dirty jeans on the washboard Ella had pointed out when she had gone back in for her clothes. Not even stopping occasionally to look up at the mimosa tree helped much any more. When her things were washed and more or less rinsed—she couldn't get the rinse water to stop being sudsy—she laid them out on the brush to dry and went back into the house and collapsed on the couch. She was feeling dizzy.

"Here, drink this," Ella said, thrusting a chipped blue-willow cup into her hands. Stacy didn't know what she was drinking, but it was cool and a little bitter and it seemed to reach to her fingers and toes. She started to get up to take the empty cup to the table, but she swayed on her feet and sat down again. She was so tired.

Ella took the cup. "You'd best rest a bit while your clothes dry." She took a pillow from under the patchwork quilt on her brass bed and put it on the couch for Stacy. The pillowcase was stiffly white and smelled like the mimosa tree.

When Stacy woke up, Nimue raised her head from her crossed paws and licked Stacy's cheek. The sun was slanting dusty rays through the window, making square patches on the wide, rough boards of the floor. Ella was at the stove, stirring something. Stacy could see the fire flickering behind the damper. She turned over on her stomach and ran her hand down Nimue's sleek back. Nimue turned over, and Stacy scratched her pink stomach. Nimue's stomach felt lumpy and swollen.

"Why is she so fat?" Stacy asked Ella, without getting up from the couch.

"She's due to whelp any day. She'll be staying

close to home now. She knows when it's her time."

"Whelp? Is something wrong with her?"

Old Ella threw a scornful glance over her shoulder but didn't stop stirring. "Doesn't anybody teach you town kids anything? She's going to have puppies."

"Oh!" Stacy was startled. She had just never thought. . . . She pulled her hand away quickly. "Barbara," she said, "is going to whelp soon, too."

"Who's Barbara?" Ella asked. She poured something from a crockery bowl into a black frying pan where it began to sizzle.

"My stepmother," Stacy answered, her voice heavy with disgust.

"Is that why you hate her?" Ella asked.

"No, of course not," Stacy said, sitting up. She thought of Barbara, her belly swollen, her arms crossed and resting contentedly on the little shelf it made. She thought of the tender, careful way her father treated Barbara now and of the time he had slapped Stacy for talking back to her. He had never slapped her before. Never in her life.

"Seems a good enough thing to be doing, having a baby. You'll think so someday, too."

Stacy felt a prickle of warmth crawling up her neck. "I don't want to have any baby, ever! I'm not going to do that!"

"Do what?"

The warmth flooded Stacy's face. "Be in bed with a man."

"A man," Ella said, shaking the skillet vigorously, "feels awful good up close, so close there's nothing could come between you."

Stacy remembered her father holding her when she was a little girl. She remembered his arms and his warm chest rising and falling with his breath. Was that what it was like for Barbara, having her father? "I'm not going to get married. I'm not going to have babies and grow big and ugly and fat."

Ella shrugged and concentrated on what was in the frying pan. Stacy could tell she thought there were worse things than growing fat with a baby . . . Stacy's father's baby. Stacy leaned over to stroke Nimue again. The dog still lay on her back, all four paws in the air.

"Not a very ladylike position," Stacy scolded in a whisper. She ran her hand down Nimue's chest and belly. Her teats were elongated from the tugging of many puppies. The bags behind them— Stacy wondered if they were called breasts on a dog—felt full. Stacy stripped one of the teats between her thumb and fingers, but no milk came. Did Barbara have milk in her breasts?

"I think it's disgusting, all of it," Stacy said to

35

Nimue, but she said it very quietly. She wondered if Ella had ever had a baby. Hard to imagine. Besides, she didn't talk about children or grandchildren. She only talked about Ben. How long ago had he died? Stacy wondered. Could having someone die be worse than having a woman around who wasn't even your mother all blown up with a baby your father had put there, wanted there, as though you weren't enough?

Nimue rolled over and got up and walked over to where her mate lay. She licked his face, starting with his muzzle and moving across one eye which he closed complacently and into his ear. The big dog groaned appreciatively.

"You'd better enjoy her attentions now, old fellow," Ella said, reaching down two plates from the cupboard next to the stove and beginning to dish up fried mush, "because in a couple of days she's going to be too busy to give you a howdy."

Stacy got up to inspect supper more closely. That was something she hadn't thought about. Once the baby came, Barbara wouldn't have time to sit at the cash register in front of the store. Stacy could sit there again, alone in the store with Daddy when there weren't any customers, and they could talk, just the way it had been before. Maybe Daddy would even do the cooking again.

Of course Stacy wouldn't be there though. That would make it all different. Daddy would surely miss her after that baby came.

Stacy took her plate and sat down at the table. Ella set a can of syrup in the middle of the table and handed Stacy the bucket from the corner. "Get some water," she said.

Before Stacy filled the bucket, she stopped to look at the mimosa tree again and to touch it. She plucked a single blossom and tucked it into her hair.

"By the way," Ella said, when Stacy had come back into the kitchen and at Ella's direction poured water into the kettle for tea, "with women you don't usually say 'whelped.' It's supposed to be different than with animals, better some way."

"Is it?" Stacy asked a little absently. She was filled again with the mimosa tree.

Ella looked at Nimue speculatively. "Who knows? It seems pretty good either way."

FIVE

"WHAT'S HIS NAME?" STACY POINTED AT THE MALE shepherd who lay just inside the doorway, watching Ella and Stacy clear their supper dishes.

"Merlin," Ella answered.

"Merlin? What a funny name. Merlin and Nimue. They're both strange."

"Don't you know Merlin?"

"No, ma'am." Where did Merlin live that she was supposed to know him?

"He's a magician . . . in King Arthur. Ben used to like him best of anybody."

"Who is King Arthur?" Stacy asked helplessly.

"Don't they teach you kids anything? When I taught school I used to read to my kids from King Arthur every day. He was a king of England, a story king."

"Oh," Stacy said, taking the dish towel that Ella handed her, "then what about Nimue?"

Ella grinned, picking up a plate and dipping it

in the water she had heated on the stove. A bit of her homemade soap had made a film on the top of the water. She scoured the plate with a rag and dipped it in a second pan of clear water before handing it to Stacy. "Ben always hated Nimue, just hated her. The one in King Arthur, I mean. She's a white fairy. In the end she steals Merlin's magic and does him in, buries him anyway. Merlin can't die."

"But how do you know about King Arthur . . . and Merlin and Nimue? How did Ben know?" Stacy glanced around the simple cabin and through the open doorway at the barren landscape.

Ella handed the dishpan to Stacy. "Give the water to the tree," she said, "and then I'll show you something."

When Stacy came back in Ella was at the end of the bed leaning over a chest Stacy hadn't noticed before. "Come here," Ella directed, and Stacy looked down into the chest filled with books. "I brought them all the way from Arkansas," Ella said, her voice filled with pride. "That's where I taught school. Ben wasn't much for reading himself, but he used to like to hear me read. When the work was done or when a blizzard would come, we would sit at the table, and I would read. I guess Ben loved King Arthur best, after the Bible. Maybe I do, too. So," she concluded, leaning on the edge of the chest to get up, "the dog is Merlin, and the bitch is Nimue."

At the sound of their names both dogs thumped the floor with their tails, but neither one moved.

Stacy bridled. "Why do you call her that?"

"Nimue?"

"No, that other word . . . bitch."

"Because that's what she is, a bitch. A bitch is a female dog."

Stacy flushed and turned away. She remembered whispered voices in her father's store. Why did they think they could say anything in front of her so long as they whispered? "That's what they used to call my mother," she said, "after she left."

"Was she?" Ella asked.

Stacy whirled around. "Of course not!"

"Then what difference does it make what they said?"

Stacy shrugged. What difference? Sitting on the stool in the dark corner of the store hearing the whispers. "I hate them all," she said.

It was Ella's turn to shrug. "That's a big load you're carrying. How far do you think you'll have to run before you get rid of it?"

"To my mother," Stacy answered. "It'll be all right when I find my mother." Now that she had already said twice that she was going to her mother, the idea sounded good.

"You'd better get started then," Ella said, sitting down on the couch with a sigh. "Your clothes must be dry by now. Why don't you go get them?"

The sky in the direction of the mesa was flame red fading into orange when Stacy got her clothes from the bushes. Her jeans and her dad's shirt were so flat and stiff they seemed to belong to some two-dimensional world.

"The iron is on the stove," Ella said, when Stacy came back in. Stacy looked down at her clothes in surprise. Was she going to have to iron them, too? She started to protest, but after a glance at Ella's face, she changed her mind. She had never ironed clothes—that was Barbara's job—but she supposed she could learn how.

The iron on the stove was an old flatiron which she had to handle with a pot holder, wetting the clothes slightly as she went, and so heavy that her arm ached in the first minute. Ella had directed her to a chest which rolled out from under the bed, and she used a sheet from there to cover the table for an ironing board.

At first steam came off the clothes in a rush, but quickly the iron cooled and refused to slide. She put it back on the stove to heat again. When she was through, she had scorched the shirt and even the sheet in several places, and the brown smell of scorched cloth filled the room. Ella didn't say anything, though.

Stacy dressed, feeling herself again in her own clothes, put away the iron and the sheet, hung Ella's dress up carefully, and went to stand in the doorway. The sky was darkening rapidly, and the first stars were beginning to be visible. The wind moaned around the corner of the house.

"I hate you, too," Stacy said, without turning away from the descending darkness.

The old woman sighed, but she didn't look up.

Stacy turned and glared at her. "Why are you making me go?" she asked.

"I'm not making you go," was the quiet reply.

"Then why did you tell me to get my clothes and get ready?"

"Because you said you wanted to go. Because you said everything would be all right when you found your mother, and you won't find your mother here."

"But why don't you try to stop me?"

"I can't stop you, Stacy. You're probably stronger than I am. And if I made you stay for now, you could just slip away when I was sleeping or walk away any time when I was busy with something else, like you did with your Dad and Barbara. How old are you, anyway?"

"Twelve," Stacy answered, shifting restlessly from one foot to the other.

"Well, that's not grown up yet, but it's a long ways from being a baby. You made up your own mind when you walked out of Cimarron City. You'll have to do the same thing here."

Stacy remained standing in the doorway. Nimue came and shoved her muzzle under her hand, and Stacy rubbed the dog's head absently, listening to the wind.

Stacy shivered and turned away from the door. "I guess I'll stay," she said, a little sullenly.

Ella was bending over a kerosene lamp she had just lit, the circle of light drawing her face sharply out of the darkness. "Hmmmph," she snorted, sharply. "I suppose I ought to be honored." She looked up at Stacy, the lamp making her cheeks and nose glow. Stacy was reminded of pictures of Halloween witches. "Have they taught you to read in that school you go to?" she asked abruptly.

"Sure," Stacy answered, with the defiance that the tone of the question seemed to demand.

"Let's see," Old Ella said, walking across to the trunk and returning with a book. She poked it at Stacy and sat down at one side of the kitchen table.

Stacy sat down at the other side and opened the book carefully, holding it down to catch the lamp light. The book was old and the pages were yellowed. "*Morte d'Arthur*," the title page said. "What's this?" Stacy asked.

"That's King Arthur, the book I was telling you about."

"Is that what *Morte* means, king?"

"No, it means death. 'The Death of Arthur.' It's French. I only went to high school, that's all you had to have to teach when I was a girl, and I didn't learn French, but I know that word."

Stacy laid the book on the table. "I don't want to read about somebody dying," she said.

Ella adjusted the wick of the lamp which had begun to send up a thin thread of smoke. "Then how about reading about somebody living? The dying only comes in the end . . . the way it will for you, too."

Stacy looked across the lamp and Old Ella smiled. "Every morning when I wake up, it's something of a surprise. Mostly a pleasant one." The darkness had filled the room, was crowding around the table. "I know, it's different when you're twelve. There's no dying when you're twelve. Don't think I don't remember. And the days stretch all around you without much difference."

Stacy turned the pages of the book very gently. She was afraid they might crumble into dust at her touch.

"Now you read," Old Ella commanded. "It's been a long while since my eyes would let me."

The lamp burned steadily, casting a white glow on the page, and Stacy began to read.

"It befell in the days of Uther Pendragon, when he was king of all England, and so reigned, that there was a mighty duke in Cornwall that held war against him long time."

Ella sighed and closed her eyes, swaying slightly in her chair to the cadence of the words.

SIX

THE NEXT MORNING WHEN STACY WOKE UP, OLD ELLA was no place in sight. Nimue was lying on the floor next to the couch, but Merlin wasn't there either. Stacy sat up and rubbed her eyes and unwrapped herself from the tangle of the blanket in which she had been sleeping. The sun was coming through the kitchen window brightly and the morning was already hot. Stacy went to the outhouse, which was off a ways on the kitchen side of the house. Though she circled the tree and the house, which were the only obstacles to vision in the cup of prairie in which Ben had built, she saw no one. Nimue followed her, ploddingly, everywhere she went but settled back to her place on the floor and puffed air through her nostrils with an enormous sigh when they came back into the house.

Stacy knelt beside her and ran her hand down Nimue's side. She rested it on one of the bulges for a moment and this time felt a stirring under her hand. Was this what Barbara felt like with her baby, hers and Daddy's, inside of her? Stacy pressed her hand for a moment on her own flat belly. It was hard to imagine! A baby growing in there! She rubbed the back of her hand over the bumps of her sprouting breasts. One was larger than the other, had started months sooner—she worried sometimes that the other wouldn't ever catch up—and they ached once in a while, with the growing she supposed, and of course she hated them. But still . . . if you had a baby, your own baby, you could feed it . . . yourself.

Stacy got up and checked the table. Ella had left a plate of cold fried mush, left over from last night, and the syrup was out. There was sweet tea, too.

Old Ella appeared in the doorway before Stacy was through eating. She was carrying a jackrabbit by its hind legs. It hung limply from her hand, its huge ears trailing the ground. Merlin stood just behind her waiting for her to move all the way in from the doorway before he entered.

"We'll have meat tonight," Old Ella said. "Wish it was something tastier than jackrabbit, but the traps don't get much else these days." As she moved across the kitchen, thumping her cane on the floor, Merlin came in. He drank loudly from the pan of water that was always set for the dogs at the head of the bed and crunched a few mouthfuls of dry dog food before he thunked down on the floor, panting loudly.

"Makes me feel good to still be going when he tuckers out," Ella commented, taking a long butcher knife from the cupboard. "They're like me, both of them, not so young any more. I'll keep one of the bitches, maybe from this litter or the next. Nimue probably shouldn't have pups many more years, and if she quits having pups, I quit eating, except what I can get from my traps. Her pups get a hundred dollars apiece in Amarillo. She always has eight or nine. That does me for the year, that and the money I get leasing this homestead to Mr. Henderson."

"When will you be going to town again?" Stacy asked, still wondering how long it would be before Old Ella turned her in as a runaway.

"Not for a couple of months, when Nimue's pups are ready to go. Mr. Henderson takes me to Amarillo with him about every three months. He lives right along the mesa, about five miles north and west of here."

"Does he come by here often?" Stacy asked casually, walking to the doorway where Ella now stood with the knife and the rabbit and gazing along the mesa.

Ella shook her head and sat down on the door-sill. She laid the knife down and picked up an ax. "At least once a month. He was just here a few days ago, so I don't suppose we'll see him for a while."

Good, Stacy thought. That's good. But she wasn't sure if she was relieved or disappointed.

Ella laid the rabbit down and with a single swift stroke chopped off the head. Stacy turned away, but then couldn't resist looking again. The rabbit head looked like a mistake, lying in the sand next to the doorsill, one eye staring in Old Ella's direction. Ella took up the carcass and the knife, made a slit in the back, inserted her fingers and pulled the skin off quickly and neatly as though she were undressing a doll. The tail looked like a fuzzy, black flag. When she slit the carcass and began dividing the entrails between the dogs, Stacy turned away again and walked over to the stove, swallowing hard.

Old Ella grinned over her shoulder at Stacy. "Are you going to enjoy rabbit tonight, or are you going to have more cold mush?"

"I don't know," Stacy replied, taking a deep breath.

"I'll make a guess, after you've smelled him cooking for a while, you'll have rabbit." Ella chuckled. "Too bad I don't have an onion to stuff him with. I used to keep a garden when Ben was here. For quite a while afterwards, too. Ate better then. But I finally got so I couldn't carry that much water. Even when I carried water regular, I'd lose a lot of the garden to the heat or the rabbits or hail or gully-washing rains. I gave up on gardens. The dogs take care of me now. The dogs and Henderson."

Stacy picked up her dishes and took them to the stove to wash. "Is your husband, I mean is Ben, is he. . . ."

"Dead? Not so far as I know. He's more like your mother, just gone, back to some greener country, no doubt. You guess the Rockies. I guess Arkansas. It's all the same."

Stacy looked up in surprise. "You mean he just left you . . . here?"

Old Ella nodded. She still had her sunbonnet on, and Stacy couldn't see her face.

"Why?"

Ella didn't say anything for a time. She got up slowly and thumped across the room and rinsed the carcass in the bucket in the corner and carried the water to the tree. After she got back, she began cutting the rabbit up. When she finally spoke, Stacy had long since ceased to expect a reply.

"This is hard country, Stacy. You've heard talk

about the dust bowl, but you can't really know what it was like. People shriveled up and died in that dryness, only some of them kept walking around."

"Was that when Ben left, during the dust bowl years?"

Ella shook her head. "No, a lot of people left then, but not Ben. If he'd given up when we had to hang wet sheets over the windows and doors to keep the dust down enough to sleep at night, I would have understood. Then maybe he would have taken me with him."

"My dad told me about the dust, too, and the wet sheets, only he was just a little boy. He thought everybody always hung up wet sheets before they went to bed."

"Did he tell you about the government coming in to shoot our cattle and then leaving them to rot?" Ella asked. "They did that during the depression. People starving and we could hardly stay for the stink of the rotting meat."

Stacy wrinkled her nose as though she could smell the meat. "Why did you let them?" she asked.

Ella cut the jackrabbit's back in half with a scrunching of bone. "The government paid to shoot them. You didn't get anything if a cow died from lack of water and grass."

"When *did* Ben leave then?"

"During the fifties, when the buffalo grass had come back and the fight was over, when we could see we would never have much on this little spread but that what was here was ours. He got an itch, and he went tagging after the oil wells, working for one of those big companies."

"And he never came back?"

"Once or twice, with a paycheck and the filth from the wells ground into his skin. He'd always been such a clean man, tall and straight and clean. He hated the wells, too, like he cursed the land he'd taught me to love." Ella piled the pieces of the rabbit together on the end of the cold stove. It looked like any kind of meat now.

"He'd begun to change. He was restless and angry, wanting something. Something that wasn't here. Maybe if . . ." Ella's voice faltered and stopped. The deep sunbonnet hid her face as effectively as a mask. She shook her head slowly from side to side, then drew in her breath. "But no, there's never any going back to change things. You just live with what the Lord brings you . . . each day."

"Even when it's a husband that runs off and leaves you?"

Ella looked squarely at Stacy. "Well, child, is there any other way?"

"Yes, you could send the sheriff after him,

make him come back."

Ella seemed to grow taller. Her voice was fierce. "Nobody stays with me without wanting to. Even the dogs are free to leave if they choose. Even you are!"

Stacy sighed. She put away the dishes she had washed and carried her water out to Old Ella's "wedding tree," heavy with flowers. The tree bloomed, never knowing that the man who planted it was gone. When she came back in, Stacy said, "But don't you just hate him?"

"Hate him?" Ella looked up speculatively, her voice soft again. "I suppose I did at first. I cried and I blamed him and I blamed myself and I wanted to die for shame and I wanted him to die instead, just to show him. But that was twenty-five years ago, nearly."

Stacy sat down at the table and watched as Ella put wood in the stove and dry brush to start the fire and then lit it. It didn't seem that she was going to say anything more, so finally Stacy prodded, "But you don't hate him now?"

Ella took off her sunbonnet and took it to hang behind the curtain in the corner of the bedroom. She shook her head and smoothed down her apron. "What use would it be?"

"It could make you feel better!"

"Could it?" Ella put a black, cast-iron frying

pan on the stove and scooped some lard into it with a wooden spoon. She stood with her back to Stacy, stirring the melting fat with great concentration. When she began talking again, it was with a sharp intake of breath, the words expelled in a kind of sing-song, as though she were reciting an ancient legend about some stranger, about some Arthur or Lancelot, instead of talking about herself.

"One morning I got up and dried my pillow and said, 'Ella, what are you staying for? Why don't you go, too?' And I went out and I looked at the sky and at the soft prairie colors stretching on as far as a person can look, and I felt the breathing room that was what first brought us here.

"I listened to the wind singing the same as it sang through the covered wagons." Ella looked up from the stove, out the little four-paned window next to the cupboard. "You know, you can walk along the Santa Fe trail just about a mile from here; six wagons abreast it was through here, and they cut a trail so deep it's still there.

"I felt that wind on my face, and I knew it was too late for me to leave. The land had me."

She held her hand over the pan, feeling the heat. "Ben did what he had to do. He painted checkerboards one whole winter while he waited for me because he hated it so, but he stuck it out for most of twenty-five years because it was ours, his and mine. He taught me to trap and to garden and to birth the calves. He gave me what I needed to live out here. And all I had to give him was stories out of books. I thought that would be enough. I was wrong."

"And so you quit hating, just like that?" Stacy asked. "You looked at the sky and the prairie and probably that silly tree, and you didn't hate him any more?" Stacy was angry, but she didn't know why. The anger rose in her chest and made her words come out sharp and tight.

Old Ella held a piece of rabbit over the pan, waiting for the lard to be hot. "No. The quitting took a long time. And I had to work at it some. Just like you'll have to work on not hating your mother."

Stacy stood up so abruptly that her chair clattered over. "I don't hate my mother!" she shouted. "Where did you ever get a stupid idea like that? It's not the same at all, my mother and Ben. It's completely different!"

"Is it?" Ella asked, without turning around.

"Yes!" Stacy shouted, and she picked up her chair and shoved it up against the table and headed for the door. Merlin followed her outside.

Old Ella called after her. "If you're going to run

away, you might take some water this time."

Stacy stopped abruptly and scowled at the ground. Merlin sat down and leaned against her leg. Stacy scratched his head, and he grumbled comfortably in his throat. Stacy grinned. Merlin liked her! She sat down and threw her arms around his big shoulders. "I'm not running away," she answered into the sleek white fur.

SEVEN

THERE WAS RABBIT FOR SUPPER AND A RICH, BROWN
gravy and rice and biscuits. The meat was stringy,
but the gravy and rice and biscuits were del-
icious. During the afternoon Stacy and Ella had
dragged a bale of straw from the outhouse and
broken it open in the corner between the end of
the couch and the wall for Nimue's whelping
bed. Nimue had gone to it immediately, scratched
around in it, turned around several times and lain
down. She lay now in that corner with her chin on
her paws, watching Stacy and Ella. Neither dog
ever came near the table while they were eating.

Merlin rose first from where he had been lying
next to Ella's bed and padded softly to the doorway, his nails clicking on the worn boards. He
stood watching and sniffing the air, his sensitive
ears cupping the prairie sounds . . . or something
more than the prairie sounds. Nimue got up and
moved into place beside him. In another minute

Stacy could hear it, too, a motor, grumbling and jolting. She laid down her fork and shot a quick glance at Ella, who was still eating. "Somebody's coming," she said.

Ella looked over at the dogs. "I know."

Stacy began to feel frightened, as though she were caught in a trap. She stood up. "Who could it be?"

"Must be Henderson," Ella said, wiping up the gravy from her plate with a biscuit, "else the dogs would be barking."

"But you said he usually comes once a month, that he was here just a few days ago."

"Usually," Ella agreed amiably.

"Well then, what is he doing back here now?" Stacy's voice was sharp, accusing.

"Don't know. I suppose he has a reason though."

"He'll find me!"

Ella looked at Stacy inquiringly, her brown face crisscrossed with tiny lines. "Is Henderson looking for you?"

"I ran away from home, remember? Everybody's looking for me!"

Ella stood up and picked up her empty plate and headed for the stove. "Not quite everybody, I don't suppose."

Stacy felt a new surge of anger now instead of

fear. Ella didn't think it mattered, her running away; she probably didn't think even her father and Barbara cared. "You crazy old woman. You could be put in jail. I ran away, and you're help-ing me. That's against the law, you know. Both of us, we're against the law."

"Well then, unless you want a ride back into town, you'd best not give Mr. Henderson your life history."

Stacy could hear the clatter of a pickup, then the clatter stopped, and the motor, and she heard the sharp slam of a door.

"Are you going to lie?" she asked.

"Don't see any reason why I should."

"But what if he asks?"

"Stacy, people came to this country because they wanted a little peace, some separation. They don't ask. You offer what you've a mind to."

The dogs started out the door, their tails wag-ging. Stacy picked up her plate and headed for the stove. "I'll redd up the dishes," she said to Ella in a low voice. Maybe if she stayed back in the cor-ner, Ella would meet Henderson outside and keep him from coming in.

A figure loomed in the doorway, tall as the door, skinny and slightly bent. "Howdy, Ella. I brought you your rheumatism medicine." Mr. Henderson held up a narrow brown sack, which he held by the top, revealing the shape of a bottle.

Ella snorted. "You mean *your* rheumatism medicine, Mr. Henderson. You know I've got no more rheumatism than a baby."

The man grinned, revealing tobacco-stained teeth, and pulled a bottle of whiskey out of the sack. The label said Early Times. Stacy knew it was whiskey. She had seen it at home lots of times before her mother . . . She turned toward the stove and began to busy herself dipping hot water into the enameled pan. She wouldn't look at Mr. Henderson, then maybe he would go away.

"I know, old lady," he said, "you just hobble around with that cane for the dignity it gives you and as protection from rattlers. But what rattler would be foolish enough to bite the likes of you, I'll never know. Anyway, I 'spect you won't mind sharing a bit of it with me so that *my* aching joints feel better."

"Why don't you go home and drink with your wife, Henderson?"

"Now, Ella. You know that Sadie's a right Christian woman and believes on the Bible and all—all except the part where Paul tells Timothy to take a little wine for his stomach. I never could get her to stand on that text. You got some glasses?" He pulled a chair out and sat down at the table, taking his straw hat off and putting it on the floor beside his chair.

"Well," Ella said, "I suppose I might have a touch of rheumatism at that." She sat down opposite him at the table. "Stacy, bring two glasses."

Stacy hesitated at the stove. She could hardly pretend she hadn't heard. Was Ella going to get drunk? Were she and this old man going to sit there and get drunk? A swift vision filled her, her mother pouring from a bottle like that, over and over, her mother with her hair disheveled, her face flushed with something more than the constant heat, stumbling a little and slopping things on the stove as she tried to cook dinner. She would curse quietly to herself, and then finally she would cry. When Stacy put her arms around her, her mother would stroke her hair and chant, like a small child, "Look at me. I used to be a pretty girl, now look at me." And nothing Stacy might try to say seemed to help. Stacy reached the glasses and carried them over to the table, thunking them down next to the bottle.

"Henderson, this is Stacy. She's visiting me."

Mr. Henderson held out a huge brown hand which swallowed Stacy's tentatively offered small one. "Howdy," he said.

"Excuse me, ma'am," Stacy said, turning away

from the bearer of whiskey and looking at Ella, "but may I get the Arthur book and read to myself some?"

Ella nodded. Mr. Henderson was pouring a bit of the amber liquid into each glass. It smelled sweet, but sharp at the same time. It smelled like Stacy's mother's kisses. Stacy got the book from the trunk and sat on the couch, on the end farthest away from Old Ella and Mr. Henderson.

While Stacy read, the words often blurring on the page in her concentration to avoid the conversation of the two at the table, Ella and Mr. Henderson talked and sipped their whiskey. They seemed, in fact, Stacy decided, a far sight more interested in talking than they were in drinking. When Mr. Henderson got up to go, they hadn't poured a second drink. He left the bottle on the table.

"You'd best take your rheumatism medicine, Jack."

"Ella, it would be a sin to have Sadie pour good whiskey down the kitchen sink. You keep it here in case you ever miss with that cane and get snake bit . . . or if you do develop a touch of rheumatism."

"I'll keep it here," Ella answered, "in case some old codger comes by needing some talk."

Mr. Henderson bent down and picked up his hat. "Pleased to have met you, Stacy," he said, bowing in Stacy's direction. She nodded back, still a little stiffly. In the doorway he turned, pointing a gnarled finger at Ella. "You'd better watch what codgers you share that with, now. A girl like you has her reputation to consider."

"Oh, you!" Ella shooed him with her apron and he was gone. She stood just inside the doorway, her face pensive, her lips faintly smiling. Then she sighed. "Jack Henderson's a good one," she said to Stacy without turning from the doorway. "He finds any excuse in the world, just to come by and check." She stood watching as Stacy heard the pickup door slam and the motor roar into life. When Stacy couldn't hear the motor any more, Ella added, softly, "It's good just to hear a man's voice."

Stacy came and stood next to Ella, *Morte d'Arthur* tucked comfortably under her arm, and watched the dust settle where the pickup had been. Why did every small leavetaking make her sad?

"And you don't hate Ben . . . for being gone?"

Ella sighed deeply, but she didn't answer, and she didn't move out of the doorway.

"You hate him, don't you?" Stacy persisted. Why did she have to probe the old woman's pain? What did Ben have to do with her?

"Sometimes . . . ," Ella answered very quietly, "sometimes I wake up in the night, even now, and reach out to the other side of the bed to touch him. When my hand finds he isn't there . . ." Silence was heavy between them. The wind whistled around the corner of the house. Darkness pressed in from every side. "Almost, Stacy . . . almost it feels like hating, just for that moment, in the night."

Stacy looked over at the old woman who stood very erect in the doorway. She laid her hand on her arm. She could feel Ella's bones. "I think I know what you mean," she said.

They moved together to the table, and Ella lit the lamp and Stacy read of King Arthur's beloved friend, Lancelot. The bottle of whiskey, mostly full, stood on the table between them.

Ella had been sleeping for some time, snoring softly. Stacy sat up and curled her legs under herself, nestling into the sag in the middle of the couch. A pale, young moon shone in the window at the foot of the couch. Stacy thought she could see the whiskey bottle glint in the light of it.

Stacy and her father had never talked about her mother's drinking, though Stacy had heard them argue about it.

"Stop," he would say. "Look what you're doing to yourself. You've got to stop."

"I can't," her mother would whimper. "I try. I

really do, but I can't." And then she would cry. Stacy would hear her cry through her bedroom walls, and she would cover her head with her pillow.

But Ella and Mr. Henderson stopped. They had one drink and they talked and their hands didn't shake and Mr. Henderson had walked out as straight as he walked in. And the bottle still sat there. No one had touched it. Why couldn't it have been that easy with her mother?

Once Stacy had been asking her father, for the hundredth time, "Why, Daddy? Why did she leave us?" and his face had twisted and he had slammed his fist down on the table, making all the dishes jump, and he had shouted, "I don't know why. Because she was a drunk. Because she cared more for drinking than for you and me. To hell with why. To hell with her!" Stacy had never asked about her again, and not long after that Barbara had come. Was that what her father was saying about Stacy now, "To hell with her"?

"Am I like my mother?" she whispered in the direction of the glint of the bottle. She had to know. She moved very quietly across the room, picked up the bottle from the table, and went through the door. She was sitting down with her back to the trunk of the mimosa tree before she began to breathe again. She had left the cabin so quietly that neither dog had awakened to follow her.

The moon made leaf shadows all around her, but it gave only the faintest light. When she had opened the bottle and lifted it to fill herself with the pungent mother-smell, she couldn't smell the mimosa any longer. She put the bottle to her lips and tipped it cautiously. The whiskey burned her mouth and took her breath away. She choked. She got the next sip down without choking, but her eyes stung and it still burned in her stomach. Ella and Mr. Henderson had sat there across the table from one another, drinking it without any difficulty. Maybe a person could get used to it in time. Stacy took another sip. It tasted terrible. Perhaps if she kept trying.

After a time—the slivered moon had set so there were no leaf shadows any longer—Stacy reached up to touch her nose. Her finger missed the first time. When she had located her nose, it still felt as though it weren't there. Stacy stood up, but the ground wouldn't stay firm beneath her. It undulated in slow, uneven waves. Her foot struck against something smooth and hard, and she heard the whiskey gurgling out of the bottle onto the ground. "Oh, my mother. My poor mother," she said to the whiskey stench, and she thought she could feel tears on her face. Then she was sick.

She made her way back to Ella's couch without noticing how she got there.

EIGHT

THE LIGHT COMING IN THE WINDOW HURT STACY'S eyes. It hurt her head, too, like a weight too heavy to be endured. She closed her eyes and buried her face in the pillow. Her mouth tasted like old socks. Then she heard again the groan that had awakened her. She sat up, closing her eyes for a moment to fight back the pain in her head, and then steadied herself on the arm of the couch to stand up.

Old Ella was gone. Merlin, too. Nimue was lying on her side in the whelping bed, and she groaned again.

"Oh, Nimue," Stacy said, kneeling beside her, the headache forgotten, "is it time?" Nimue stood up, turned around restlessly, scratching at the straw and lay down again. Her sides drew in tightly and relaxed. She looked at Stacy as though she expected something.

The panic began to rise in Stacy's throat. She looked around. Leave it to Old Ella to go off somewhere when Nimue was about to whelp. Where was she? She must be walking the traps again, Merlin with her. Where were the traps? Stacy had not even asked. Nimue was beginning to breathe heavily. "Wait here," Stacy said, as though Nimue might be going somewhere, "I'll find her."

She ran to the door and looked out at the empty prairie, empty as the day the first settlers crossed it. She looked back at Nimue, whose eyes had followed her, then ran out the door. The first direct sunlight hit her like a blow, and she was aware again of the pounding in her head. She ran up the slope to the rim of the bowl, but though the prairie rose and fell before her for many miles, she could see no sign of Ella, no flash of white that would be Merlin. She walked the rim and then hurried back into the house. She and Nimue were alone.

Nimue was standing in her straw bed. She whined when she saw Stacy and lay down again. She was beginning to pant. Was anything wrong? Nimue had had puppies before. Wild animals took care of themselves. Would a dog need tending? Nimue whimpered, and her sides contracted. She partly rose, nuzzled and licked her vagina, and flopped back down. She groaned, and her eyes were on Stacy.

"Nimue, what do you need?" Stacy felt frantic. She looked around as though this time she might see Old Ella there. She was alone. A white, mucusy substance, tinged with red, oozed out and Nimue licked it away. Nimue lay back down and she groaned and shuddered with another contraction. Surely it wasn't supposed to be so hard. What if she needed help? What could Stacy do?

Her hands needed to be clean. Stacy jumped up to go to the water bucket. Nimue struggled to her feet, but Stacy stroked her head and told her to lie down. She lay down with a deep sigh. Stacy poured some water from the bucket into the enameled tin bowl and scrubbed her hands with the yellow soap. "Like a doctor getting ready for surgery," she mocked herself. Her voice sounded hollow, as though it echoed from the stone walls. She and Nimue might have been alone in the world.

She went back to Nimue, who was lying on her side, panting heavily. Her eyes were beginning to be glazed. "Nimue. Nimue. What's wrong?" Stacy crawled along the side of the whelping bed, running her hand along Nimue's side as she moved. The lumps and bumps were still there. Nimue's sides contracted again and then relaxed. More mucus oozed out, but Nimue didn't clean herself this time. Another contraction and she started up with a little yelp then lay back down with a faint whimper.

"Let me see, Nimue." Stacy lifted her back leg carefully. The dog's vagina was swollen and stretched open a little. She could see a grayish white membrane. Was that a puppy? Or was it part of Nimue? If it was supposed to come out, she could help it. But what if she hurt Nimue? Stacy got up and climbed over the corner of the couch to run for the door. She looked out helplessly, already knowing that Old Ella would be nowhere in sight. A pocket gopher scurried past the door. Nimue let out a squeal of real pain, and Stacy hurried back to the dog, who raised her head and looked at Stacy beseechingly. Nimue got up, turned around frantically several times, snapped at her own tail, and settled down again with a groan.

"Nimue, Nimue. Tell me how I can help," Stacy whispered. Nimue answered with another squeal that made Stacy's stomach wrench. She knelt beside her, lifted her leg again and touched the gray sack that protruded a little farther now. It was slippery and she drew her hand away involuntarily. Nimue raised her head to look back at Stacy and her eyes were filled with such trust that Stacy reached out again and touched the sack. Was Nimue dying? Stacy gritted her teeth and pushed against the gray membrane, tucking it back in. If that grayish sack was a puppy, it would come out still; if it wasn't . . . she shuddered and wiped her hand on her jeans. Nimue seemed more relaxed for a moment. With the next contraction again the gray sack began to emerge. This time Stacy could make out a pink nose through the membrane. It was a puppy, a real puppy. Nimue whimpered. She checked herself, tried to get up, flopped down and let out a strangled cry.

As the contraction finished, the puppy began to disappear back into the vagina. Stacy reached for it. She had to help. The sack that enclosed the puppy was slippery. She couldn't get a hold under the puppy's jaw. She put two fingers of her other hand behind its head from the top and pulled. Nimue screamed and pulled away from her. Another contraction began and Stacy was pulling down now. The puppy practically popped out into Stacy's hand. Nimue sighed deeply and didn't lift her head to see her new baby. Stacy sat there, holding the still-enclosed little being in her hand, examining its form through the walls of its sack, and her heart pounded and she bit her lips to stop their trembling.

After a moment her relief passed into horror. Surely Nimue should be doing something for this puppy. It hadn't begun to breathe. It couldn't breathe as long as it was in the gray sack. Nimue lay still, breathing deeply, recovering from the pain and the effort of the difficult birth. Stacy tore at the sack with her fingernails, but it was tough and she couldn't even make a tear. She could see the slits of the puppy's closed eyes, its tiny pink nose through the wall that still separated it from the world. She sprang up and ran for the cupboard where she had seen Ella put the knife. Returning with the knife, she knelt over the puppy, pulled at some of the membrane, and slit it carefully. When she pulled the sack down over the puppy's damp, furry head, it opened its pink mouth and gasped for breath. Tears ran down Stacy's cheeks, but she wasn't crying. Stacy prided herself in never crying.

Nimue finally roused herself and chewed off the umbilical cord, which was attached to a dark red, liverish-looking substance which had followed on the next contraction. That would be the placenta. Stacy had studied about babies in her health class at school, and she knew about the placenta and the way all baby animals, even humans, received nourishment through it before they were born. Nimue ate the placenta, in the matter-of-fact way of dogs, and proceeded to lick her first puppy dry, tumbling him—Stacy now saw it was a male—over with her nose in the rough-gentle manner of experienced mothers. He was perfectly white, like both his parents, with a miniature triangle of a nose and tiny pink pads on his paws and even perfect tiny claws.

Soon Nimue lay back and the contractions began again. Stacy bit her lips and held her breath for a moment, but soon another puppy emerged easily, isolated and fragile-looking in its casing, wiggling and squirming, grunting and squeaking its way to Nimue's teats as soon as she had torn off the sack with her teeth and licked life into it. Him, it was another male. The first puppy wasn't nursing, but persisted in burrowing in that warm, moist area from which he had come, as though after his difficult entry into the world he wanted only to return to the first warmth and security he had known.

While Stacy sat on the floor and watched, the morning slipping by unnoticed, six more puppies were born, all perfectly white, four more males and two females. Stacy felt Nimue's sides. She seemed to be caved in. There were no more puppies. Nimue lay back with a pleased air, sustained for the moment by the afterbirth she had eaten after each puppy, her puppies and her bed clean, and nursed her pups. They wiggled and grunted, sucked vigorously, lost their hold and burrowed blindly after another teat, pushed one another, occasionally sucked for a moment on one another's pink ears that were tightly folded against their heads. Nimue raised her head to lick them from time to time, to nuzzle among them, to look them over as though she said, "Look what I did." Only the first puppy was still not nursing. He would burrow and grunt with the others, but he never seemed to take hold.

Stacy picked him up and stroked his head with one finger. She felt as though this little puppy had been born to her. It was incredible, this live creature, formed so exquisitely, so perfectly, had grown hidden inside his mother and now was here, in her hand. The pup raised his blind face toward Stacy, waving unsteadily, and sniffed. Stacy had already decided to name this special puppy after King Arthur's companion.

"You don't know me, Lancelot," she said, "but I'm your friend. I'm the one who got you here. With a little help from your mother, of course," she acknowledged, patting Nimue's side. The puppy opened its pink mouth soundlessly, and that was the first time Stacy noticed, an opening, almost a crack through the puppy's upper lip and back deep into the roof of his mouth.

Stacy touched the open lip with her finger. Was that why he wasn't sucking? She picked up one of the other males who had for the moment gone to sleep crossways over the top of three of his brothers and turned him onto his back. He wriggled and opened his mouth in a startled, squeaking cry. He had no opening in his lip. Stacy looked again at Lancelot. The dark opening came almost to his nose. Something was wrong with Lancelot! Something was wrong with the puppy she had saved!

Nimue growled deep in her throat. Stacy whirled to look behind her. Merlin was standing with only his front paws through the open door-way. Hearing Nimue's warning, he came no farther. Stacy laid the two puppies down carefully next to Nimue.

"Ella, Ella," she called, running for the door. But when she got to the doorway, no one was there except Merlin, who whined, danced back and forth, and started up the hill.

NINE

STACY HESITATED IN THE DOORWAY. MERLIN HAD reached the top of the rise; he looked back and ran halfway down the hill. He sat down, cocked his head, and whined impatiently. Old Ella was nowhere in sight. Something must have happened to her. Stacy glanced back at Nimue, who was resting comfortably in her corner, then she started out, avoiding the tree and the empty bottle she knew was there. As soon as Merlin saw she was following him, he disappeared over the hill. When Stacy got to the top of the rise, he was waiting about fifty feet ahead. He started moving again, looking back over his shoulder frequently to make sure Stacy was following, stopping and waiting with his head cocked at an impatient angle when she got too far behind.

Obviously something was wrong. Ella should have been back to the cabin hours before. Stacy had been so occupied, once the puppies had started to come, that she had scarcely thought about her, but something must have happened to her. Stacy paused on a rise to catch her breath. She hadn't picked up her hat before she had started out, and the sun was heavy on her scalp. She looked around. The mesas and buttes rose, craggy, on ahead of her. There was nothing but prairie between her and them, no place for Old Ella to be. Where was Merlin leading her?

A buzzard was circling on ahead, two, three. Merlin turned back and barked, a short, deep command, and then he ran on, dropping into a ravine so quickly that Stacy almost lost sight of him before she realized where he was going. She followed quickly and was soon into the river breaks, dropping down into a canyon so narrow that from a slight distance it was possible to look across it without even knowing it was there. Partway down the canyon, covering the path so that Stacy had to hold her breath and edge around it, was the carcass of a cow. The buzzards circled overhead and then flew off to circle farther below. At the bottom of the canyon, Old Ella sat leaning against a rock, flailing her cane in the direction of the buzzards. A shadow passed over Stacy and she ducked instinctively.

"Damned buzzards!" Old Ella shouted hoarsely. "Stupid birds! Don't know a live woman from a dead cow."

"Ella," Stacy called, "are you all right?" She ran and knelt next to the old woman.

"Of course I'm not all right," Ella answered. "Do you think I would be sitting here in the sun in the middle of the day if I was all right? Help me up, girl. It's my ankle. I guess I must have hit my head, been out for a time, so Merlin just lies here next to me like a headstone. Wouldn't go back without being told."

Stacy reached out to touch the boot Ella had indicated—there was no way with it on to see what was wrong—and Ella rapped her knuckles with her cane. "Leave it alone. Just help me home. Can't do anything for it out here anyway." Merlin was sitting between them, panting, his tongue lolling, apparently satisfied with the results of his mission. "Ought to ask you the same question. You all right? I noticed you fed Henderson's whiskey to my tree. A bit to yourself, too, I'd guess."

Stacy felt herself flush. "I'm fine. I . . . I . . . about the whiskey. . . ."

Ella waved her words away. "Save it for Henderson," she said.

Stacy helped Old Ella to her feet. "What happened to that cow?" she asked, changing the subject.

Ella shrugged. "It died, the way all creatures do one time or another."

"But why?" Stacy was looking for a path out of the canyon that didn't go near the carcass, but there didn't seem to be one.

Ella's tone was wry. "Old age most likely."

Stacy put one arm around Old Ella's waist. Her bones felt fragile. If she squeezed too hard, the little old woman would probably shatter. She supported Ella's elbow with her other hand. Her skin felt dry and papery. Ella leaned heavily on Stacy, barely touching the injured foot to the ground, and they made their way slowly out of the river breaks, leaving the carcass and the sandy riverbed behind. The distance which had been short in coming was long in returning. Ella didn't speak, and Stacy knew something of the extent of her pain only by the way the air whistled between her teeth sharply if a movement jolted her. As they walked, Stacy talked, telling her about the puppies, about the first difficult birth, about the way she had been able to help. The excitement of it all still pulsed through her.

"They're so marvelous," Stacy finished, "so . . . so alive and real. They have everything, noses and claws and tails. And when they yawn, their mouths are so pink! I didn't know it was like that . . . babies, I mean. For something so *finished* to come out of the mother."

Ella nodded. "It's good you were there."

Whom did she mean it was good for, her or Nimue? Well, it didn't matter. Stacy was glad she had been there to help, glad for herself and glad for Nimue, too. Thinking about the puppies, she remembered what she had forgotten, the opening, like a crack, in the mouth of the first little male. Slowly, struggling for words, she told Ella about the opening, about the fact that that pup wasn't nursing.

Ella didn't answer at first, and then when Stacy was about to say it again, thinking somehow that she hadn't heard, Ella said, "We'll have to see about it when we get there."

In the cabin Nimue rose to greet them, tumbling her puppies over one another, and the puppies began to cry as they nosed their blind way through the straw. Seeing Ella and giving a welcoming wag, Nimue lay down again, nuzzling her pups. She gave the barest growl in her throat when Merlin appeared in the doorway. He did not come in.

Stacy helped Ella to her bed and then gently, taking off her starched bonnet and laying it aside first, she began unlacing her boot. Ella's ankle emerged already swollen and purple. Even unlaced, the boot came off with difficulty, and Ella drew in her breath so sharply with the pain of removing the boot that Stacy almost cried out herself.

"Did you fall off something?" Stacy asked, returning at Ella's direction with a towel dipped in cold water to wrap the ankle.

"Nope. Just stepped off a rock and the foolish ankle gave out on me. That's the trouble with getting old. Your body quits."

"Do you think it's broken?" Stacy asked.

"Nope. Too mean."

"What's too mean?"

"I am. Too mean to break anything. It's just turned. A little time in bed. Get me a drink of water and then take off my other boot before it dirties the quilt."

Stacy brought the water and then bent to unlace the other boot, watching Ella's face out of the corner of her eye. She looked gray, and her lips were pulled tightly over her teeth.

"I think I'd better get somebody," Stacy said, setting the boot next to the other and carrying the bonnet to the "closet" behind the curtain.

"Not time now," Ella answered. "Later you can go get Henderson. He's just five miles along Black Mesa, that way." She pointed north and west. "Now we need to tend to Nimue and the pups. Did you give her fresh water?" Stacy shook her head.

"Well do that, and then we'll check them over."

Stacy carried the pan of water over to Nimue,

who drank and settled back in the straw with a deep sigh.

"Did the afterbirth come with each puppy?" Ella asked. "That's important, because she'll be sick if it didn't."

Stacy nodded. She brought the puppies to Old Ella one at a time, starting with the two females and saving Lancelot for last. Ella examined each puppy carefully and nodded with satisfaction. Nimue raised her head to watch them and licked each puppy as Stacy returned it to her bed. Lancelot had crawled off into the far corner of the bed by himself. Stacy picked him up gently.

"I've named this one," she said to Old Ella as she handed her the puppy. "He's Lancelot."

Old Ella looked the puppy over very slowly and carefully, turning him in her hand and finally opening the tiny mouth with one finger to examine the opening.

She sighed. "That's what I thought. He has a cleft palate. We'll have to take care of him."

Relief washed over Stacy. "Then he'll be all right?"

Ella shook her head. "That's not what I mean. He's going to die. He'll starve to death if we leave him, because he can't suck. Even if we had an eye-dropper and milk—and I don't have either—we couldn't keep him alive. He needs to be taken care of now, before he begins to suffer."

Ella lay back on her pillow and closed her eyes, the puppy still cupped in her hands. Her face was beginning to look white, the thin skin drawn tight across her cheekbones. "Go draw a bucket of water from the spring. Leave it outside the door."

Stacy stood by Ella's bed, shifting her weight, trying not to comprehend.

"I'll walk over to Mr. Henderson's with him. He could take us to the vet in Cimarron City. The vet could do something."

Ella shook her head heavily. "There's nothing the vet can do, Stacy." Her eyes remained closed. In fact, she was so still, immersed apparently in her own pain, that she hardly seemed to be breathing.

Stacy watched her for a moment, but she wasn't seeing Ella, she was seeing Nimue while Lancelot was being born, hearing her cries of pain. She had forgotten, after the thrill of his birth and the other easier births, she had completely forgotten. She gritted her teeth. "You lied to me," she said.

Ella didn't open her eyes. "Very likely," she said. "What did I lie to you about?"

"You told me having a baby was good, that it was special."

"And . . . ?"

"And Lancelot, his being born, hurt Nimue. She cried. I was scared. It hurt bad."

Ella opened her eyes. "I told you it was good. I didn't tell you it wouldn't hurt."

"How can it be good if it hurts?"

"Is it good, being alive?"

"Yes," Stacy answered doubtfully, waiting to see what Ella was leading her into.

"Being alive hurts," Ella answered, closing her eyes again.

Stacy looked at the tiny creature, trying to lift his wavering head from Ella's cupped hands. She could see his breathing.

"Look," Ella said wearily, opening her eyes again, "this puppy is defective. He must have been weak, even before he was born. They have to help themselves to be born. Either he got caught or he was too weak to do his part, maybe both, and his mother was in pain. She was lucky. You were there to help. Maybe he wasn't so lucky."

"What do you mean?"

"Without your help, he would have been done hurting by now, dead and done hurting."

Stacy turned away to get the bucket. When she had filled it at the spring, she left it outside the door and came back in to stand by Ella's bed again. The puppy had snuggled down in Ella's hands and was sleeping. Old Ella opened her eyes.

"Stacy," she said slowly, "I'm sorry, but you have to do it. I can't get up just now, and Nimue will be upset if it's done in here where she sees."

A shudder ran through Stacy. There was no avoiding it any longer. Ella wanted her to kill the pup, to drown him! "No," she said through clenched teeth. "I won't do it."

A shadow seemed to flicker across Ella's face, but she didn't say anything except, "Here, take him," as she put the tiny bundle of soft white fur into Stacy's hands. The puppy, not just any puppy but the one Stacy had saved, Lancelot, snuggled down into Stacy's hands with little grunting sounds. Stacy raised him to her face and brushed his softness lightly against her cheek. "I'll take care of him . . . somehow."

Ella opened her eyes and looked at Stacy, her blue eyes sharp. "Fine," she said, her voice filled with disdain. "You take care of him, but not in my sight . . . or his mother's. You watch him die, hour by hour. See how many hours . . . or maybe days . . . it takes him to starve to death. Then you can feel good about yourself because you took care of him!"

"But I can't drown him!" Stacy wailed.

"Would you rather hit him on the head with a hammer or cut his head off with an ax? That's what I would do. It's quicker, easier on the creature. The drowning isn't quite over in an instant for the thing drowning. It's just easier on the person who has to do the killing. No blood. That's why I had you get the bucket, but the ax is right outside the door."

"No!" Stacy shouted.

"Then what are you going to do?"

Stacy could feel the tiny heartbeat in her hands, fluttering, incredibly fast. "You don't even care," she wailed. "They're nothing to you, nothing but money for beans and grits!"

"Huh," Ella scoffed, "after you'd been hungry for a couple of days, that nothing wouldn't be so nothing to you."

"But Lancelot is alive. I helped him be born. You can't make me kill him just because you weren't here, because he doesn't mean anything to you. He was born right into my hands!" Stacy's voice was rising to a high pitch, but she wouldn't cry. She wouldn't let Old Ella make her cry.

Ella raised herself on one elbow and glared at Stacy. A little color was coming back into her face. "You!" She spit out the word scornfully. "You always think you're the only one ever knows anything, ever feels anything. Born into your hands? Well, good for you. I had three babies, born out of my body, born with pain and with joy like you've never dreamed of, and they died, each one of them. They just sickened and died, while Ben and I watched, while I held them. Take that dog of yours and get out of here. Get where I can't see you or hear you. There's been enough suffering in this house!" Ella collapsed back on the bed and closed her eyes and turned away from Stacy.

Stacy stood for a moment, helplessly. Lancelot squirmed in her hands. Then she walked out of the cabin, holding him gently. She walked past the bucket of water she had set along the wall and around to the mimosa tree. Its fragile, brushlike blooms glowed. She sat down against the trunk, in the shade of the tree, and looked at Lancelot. He was awake again, and he opened his pink mouth wide, showing the cleft that would keep him from sucking, from living. He began to cry, and Stacy stroked him with one finger. Still he cried.

After a few moments, Stacy got up and walked to the bucket mechanically. She plunged her hand into the water, and the puppy twisted violently in her hand for an instant. When the bubbles had stopped rising to the surface of the water, Stacy lifted the limp, dripping body and held it against her breasts.

TEN

STACY DUG WITH THE SPADE SHE HAD FOUND NEXT to the outhouse. The soil, even under the mimosa tree, was dry and hard. Digging was difficult. When she had a small hole, about eight inches deep so that no wild creatures would be apt to dig up the grave, she picked up the tiny body.

The red ants that were everywhere on the summer prairie were already crawling around the closed eyes, the pink nose. The mouth hung open. Stacy had tried to close it, but it wouldn't stay. She brushed the ants off and stomped on them, but they scurried through the dust, impervious to her stamping. When she put Lancelot down again, she wouldn't be able to protect him from the ants. She took off her shirt, holding the body first in one hand, then in the other, and using her teeth to get started, tore off one sleeve and put the shirt back on. Carefully, gently, she wrapped Lancelot in the cloth of her sleeve, tucking it all around him so the ants couldn't reach him again, at least not immediately.

After she had laid him in the grave, she filled the dirt in quickly and tamped it down with the spade. The grave made a mound she could not fully tamp down.

Merlin appeared over the hill and walked slowly toward her. He moved with a quiet dignity, a beauty that made her catch her breath. Here was what Lancelot would have been like, if he had had a chance. Stacy threw the spade down and began stomping on the mound of the grave, wanting to make it disappear, wanting it to be as though none of it had happened. The ground kept the small telltale hill. She began to cry. For the first time the tears that she had hidden for so long burst forth in wracking sobs. "It's not fair," she said to Merlin. "It's not fair."

Merlin came up and nuzzled her hand, and Stacy clouted him on the side of the head. None of it was right. He was alive and strong and her puppy was dead. Killed. She had done it. Old Ella made her do it. Merlin backed off and sat down a short distance away, watching Stacy with questioning eyes.

Stacy reached up and took hold of the end of a branch and stripped leaves and blooms into her hand, dropping them, pink and green, onto the grave, leaving the end of the branch looking dead and bare. She went around the tree, stripping more and more, running back to the mound in the earth with handfuls of the tree's life. Her breath came in gasps, and she could barely see through her tears. Then she began breaking branches. She ran for Ella's hatchet and chopped and twisted and pulled, piling the living branches onto the grave until the mound had disappeared, until everything was as though the grave weren't there, until Ella's wedding tree was distorted and ugly. Finally, without stopping to look at the tree and at the mound of blooming branches, she dropped the hatchet and ran.

Stacy didn't stop running until she had dropped down into the river breaks, skirting the dead cow, turning her head away from the stench, the squirming maggots. She sat down on a pile of sandstone left standing in a small column by the erosion of the wind and buried her face in her hands. The sun made the skin on the back of her neck feel tight, but the wind cooled her. When she looked up, Merlin was sitting in front of her, his golden brown eyes searching her face.

"I'm sorry, Merlin," she whispered. "I'm sorry I hit you." Her hand trembled as she reached out to him, but he didn't draw away. She ran her hand down the heavy fur at the side of his neck. "Come with me." Stacy stood up and wiped away the last traces of her tears. "Ella doesn't need you. Come with me." Merlin followed her across the dry riverbed and on up the other side of the breaks. They headed for the mesas. The wind sang in Stacy's ears. "Run away," it seemed to say. "Run away."

Stacy didn't know where she was going. Not to her mother. She knew that much. If her mother was ever able to climb out of her whiskey bottle, maybe she would find Stacy. In the meantime, there wasn't much they could do for one another, and it didn't matter where she went. A king bird flashed past her—she caught a glimpse of its yellow breast—chasing a smaller bird and chattering in a quarrelsome manner. A shadow passed over her, and Stacy ducked again, remembering the buzzards, but when she looked up it was a black and white prairie falcon riding the wind currents, its flight a vision of joy in freedom.

"I wish we could fly," Stacy whispered to Merlin. "I wish the wind could just take us somewhere . . . anywhere." Merlin moved in beside her, his shoulder occasionally brushing against her hand. Stacy picked up a branch of pitted, dry tree cactus and hurled it ahead of them, but it didn't go very far. She crested a small hill and looked down into a prairie-dog town. A half dozen of the little sand-colored animals stood erect at the doors of their homes. Merlin was after them in a flash, swerving away from one that had disappeared and heading for another.

"Merlin," Stacy called out, agonized. Merlin dug at one of the holes for a moment, but then returned to Stacy. "Oh, Merlin, don't kill them. Don't kill anything," she pleaded. They walked on, her mind reeling slowly. What was Merlin to eat if he wasn't to kill anything? For that matter, what was she to eat? She sighed. Nothing was simple. Not parents. Not things being born. Not even a choice between living and dying. Where was she running to? She sighed again. How foolish she was being. Ella was right about her. She was just a kid who never thought about anybody else, never even thought enough about herself to act sensibly. Here she was again without any water, and this time she didn't even have her hat as protection from the sun. It was a good thing it was beginning to cloud over, getting toward evening, too.

Black Mesa cut off everything ahead of them. It wasn't so black as they got closer. Stacy could see the layers of rock like pages in a book. The wind brought dust off the mesa, ground it into Stacy's skin, threw it in her face. She walked with her hand resting lightly on Merlin's back. When she stopped to rub the dust out of her eyes, Merlin sat and waited, looking up at her, his tongue dripping. The wind was building and purple-black clouds were rolling off the mesa. Maybe it would rain. She and Merlin could use some rain. Everything could.

How Stacy's mother had hated the dust that covered everything in the store and the apartment. One of Stacy's earliest memories was of her mother, standing in the middle of their apartment with a dustcloth in her hand, crying. Had her mother found some place where the wind and dust couldn't reach her? Was that what she had been looking for?

And what was Stacy looking for? She stopped. She and Merlin had begun to climb the slope of the lower part of the mesa. She turned to face the way she had come from, Old Ella's and Cimarron City, and sat down. The sunset, which was behind the mesa, was reflected palely all around the horizon. She sat for a long time, and Merlin sat beside her, waiting.

It was nearly dark when she felt the first drops of rain. She stood up, as though from a long sleep, and looked around. She could make out the blackened mouth of a cave not far above them. "Come on, Merlin," she said, "I'm thirsty, but I'm in no mind to be washed all the way back to Ella's. Let's see who we'll be sharing the cave with. Are you afraid of rattlers?"

It was only pigeons. As they stood in the mouth of the cave, Merlin barked and a couple of dozen pigeons began squawking and stuttering, scrabbling around the cave. They swooped out over Stacy's head, but most of them flew back in again, circling confusedly before they settled. Merlin barked again and they did the same, but there were more of them this time. When they had settled a second time, Stacy called to Merlin, "Let them be. We don't need the place to ourselves."

The cave was deep and high, but Stacy stayed in the front, away from the darkness and the inevitable pigeon droppings. Merlin lay down next to her. A rumble of thunder rolled off the mesa. The rain began to fall with a singing rush. The wind quieted, and the rain lulled Stacy to sleep with Merlin as a pillow and the pigeons cooing softly from the depths of the cave.

ELEVEN

MORNING DAWNED WITH THE COOL FRESHNESS OF A rainbow. The rain had stopped during the night, but the prairie still glistened. Stacy stood in the mouth of the cave, stretching away her stiffness. She thought of Old Ella alone in her cabin. She thought of Nimue and her pups. Ella wouldn't be able to move around enough to see that Nimue got food and water. She wouldn't be able to get food and water for herself either. Stacy stood for a while, listening to a meadowlark. A mourning dove trailed its lonely call. The plains stretched in front of her endlessly, the line of the horizon sketched in charcoal. The wind sang a gentle song this morning.

"Guess we'd better go see Mr. Henderson, Merlin." Merlin wagged his tail and watched her expectantly. They started off, moving north and west along the mesa, following the directions Ella had given.

"Waill," Mr. Henderson spat a shiny brown blob of tobacco juice, "guess we'd better go take a look at Old Ella. The wife is over visiting her sister, so you and me will have to manage."

Stacy shrank inside herself. Surely he didn't expect her to go back, too, to see Ella again. Obviously he did. What could she say? No, you go on. Merlin and I are just out for a little walk. Wouldn't work. She climbed into the cab of Mr. Henderson's pickup, and Merlin jumped up in back without having to be told. They bumped in silence for a few minutes over the dirt road, the dust billowing up behind them despite last night's rain.

"Good thing for Ella you was visiting," Mr. Henderson said, shifting his tobacco to the cheek toward Stacy.

"Yes, sir," Stacy answered without inflection.

Again a silence in which they reached the paved road. Stacy thought about Ella lying alone in her small homesteader's cabin.

"I don't think she should be allowed to live by herself that way."

"Hmmmmmph," Mr. Henderson grunted, "I've never known Old Ella to need to be allowed nothing!"

"But if I hadn't been there, she might have died. She might never have gotten back to the house even. The buzzards would have eaten her."

"So . . . that's her right, ain't it?"

"To die?"

"To live the way she chooses—she's not hurting nobody out there. To die out there when the time comes. Where d'you want her to die?"

Stacy couldn't think of an answer to that.

The pickup turned off the highway, cutting through the sunflowers which lined the road, and jolting along an almost invisible track which would end at Ella's little sandstone house.

Stacy stole a look at Mr. Henderson. His face was furrowed with concentration. He was worried about Ella, too. What would Ella say when Stacy came back? Did she know about Ben's tree? "I'm sorry, Ella," she said under her breath. "I didn't mean . . ."

But she had meant it at the time. She had meant every blind stripping of leaves and flowers, every swing of the ax. She had hated Old Ella in that fierce moment. She had wanted to hurt her. Like she had wanted to hurt Barbara by running away, so that her father would blame Barbara. Like she used to wish something bad would happen to her mother and that man—a car wreck, maybe, some good reason for not coming back. The wishing was different, though. The wishing hadn't hurt her mother, just made her own insides tight and sad. Was there any way to take back Ella's hurting? Or Barbara's?

"Did you leave the whiskey where Ella could reach it?" Henderson asked suddenly. "It might help with the pain."

"No, sir," Stacy answered. "I guess I didn't." She remembered Ella saying, 'Save it for Henderson' when she had tried to explain about the whiskey. It was time to begin facing up. She looked straight ahead at the prairie.

"I . . . uh . . . I accidentally spilled the whiskey you brought Ella."

Mr. Henderson grunted something indistinguishable.

Stacy shifted uncomfortably in her seat, pulling her skin away from the plastic. "Actually, I guess I drank it . . . sort of."

"Sort of?" Mr. Henderson didn't look away from his driving.

"Well, I drank some first, then I spilled the rest. I wasn't feeling too well."

Mr. Henderson grinned and spat out the window. "Starting a little young, ain't you?"

"No, sir. I mean I'm not starting. Not ever, not unless I can stop, too. Like you and Ella. Besides it tastes awful."

"Too bad you didn't leave it for Ella," he said. "The whiskey could have helped a little."

I could have helped more, Stacy thought, but she didn't say anything. She leaned against the pickup door and sighed. They pulled up at the edge of the cup of prairie, looking down on Ella's cabin. Ella's and Ben's. Only Ben was gone. Just Ella. Just Stacy and her dad and Barbara . . . and soon the baby.

Merlin jumped down before the truck had entirely stopped moving. The truck stopped at the rim of the bowl. Stacy could see the wedding tree. It looked ragged, but the remaining blossoms still glowed. The blooms in the pile of branches were limp and brown. Had the ants found their way through the sleeve yet? She got out of the truck and approached the cabin slowly, staying well behind Mr. Henderson.

When she got to the door, Mr. Henderson was bent over examining Ella's ankle. As Stacy's eyes grew accustomed to the dusky light, she saw that Old Ella was looking at her from the bed.

"You're not much good at running away, are you?" Ella asked.

Stacy didn't answer. She just picked up the bucket and went out to the spring for water for Nimue.

Nimue drank the water loudly while Stacy fondled the puppies, which were climbing over one another and squealing in blind confusion. When Nimue lay down again, Stacy got up and poured some water for Merlin, then she got a glass from the cupboard and poured it full. As she approached the bed, Mr. Henderson straightened up from wrapping Ella's swollen ankle and hitched up his pants. "Ella, I think we'd best get you into town to the doc. He can fix you up."

Stacy supported Ella's head and shoulders and held the glass for her. Over the glass the old woman's eyes seemed to be smiling at her. "Ella," she said, and her voice caught. "Ella, I broke some of the branches from the mimosa tree."

Ella nodded, settling back onto the bed, as though she already knew. "A grave is a difficult thing to cover, Stacy." Still her eyes were smiling. "You going to stay and look after those puppies you're so taken with?"

Stacy was startled. "No, ma'am, I guess not. I think I'd best go home."

Ella's mouth smiled, too. "Might be a good idea at that," was all she said.

Stacy finished the rest of the water in Ella's glass. She hadn't realized how thirsty she was. Mr. Henderson poured out a heaping bowl of food for Nimue and one for Merlin at the door, and Stacy filled an extra bowl with water in case the doctor kept Ella in town for a couple of days. Mr. Henderson would check on the dogs if she didn't come right home.

He carried Ella out to the pickup and set her in

the front seat as gently as if she were made of glass. Stacy climbed in beside her. While they waited for Mr. Henderson to come around to the driver's seat, they sat and looked down at the torn mimosa tree and at the pile of branches.

Ella spoke so softly Stacy had to lean over to catch her words. "If even one of the babies had lived," she said, "Ben might have had reason to stay."

Stacy looked back at the tree and at the fading blooms piled onto the tiny grave. "Will it bloom next year?" she asked.

"Always has. Don't see why next year should be any different."

Mr. Henderson turned the pickup around and they bumped across the prairie. He drove slowly, trying to choose the smoothest way to keep from jarring Ella who leaned back against the seat, her eyes closed and her face gray. They rode in silence. Soon after they reached the highway, Stacy could see the grain elevator in the distance.

"Mr. Henderson," she said finally, "would you let me off at the edge of town, please. By the elevator'd be fine. I'll walk from there."

"Sure thing," he said, beginning to slow down.

Ella opened her eyes. "I've been thinking," she said, "of something you could do."

"Yes?" The truck stopped and Stacy hesitated with her hand on the door handle.

"In a year or two I'm apt to need a new bitch. Can't get pups out of Nimue forever. But if I kept one around, well, she'd be underfoot. Eat too much, too. Thought you might want to come out in a couple of months before I take the pups to Amarillo, pick one out. Keep it for me. Of course, I couldn't pay you anything."

"Oh," Stacy felt suddenly light-headed. "Oh, my. I'd have to ask Dad and Barbara, of course. But I think they would . . . if I'm . . . oh, Ella, thank you!"

"Don't thank me," Ella growled, closing her eyes and leaning her head back on the seat again. "You'd just be doing me a favor."

Stacy stood in the dust by the side of the road and watched the pickup disappear. Maybe Dad and Barbara wouldn't . . . a dog would be company for Barbara, though, when Stacy was in school . . . Barbara might get lonely staying in the apartment so much once the baby came . . . Stacy could help Daddy in the store in exchange for the food the pup would need . . . but even if they wouldn't, she'd still go back to Ella's. She had to. She'd left her hat.

AUTHOR'S NOTE

Cimarron City is an imaginary town, but the country in which it is set is very real. It is the northwestern corner of the Oklahoma panhandle, near Black Mesa. This ruggedly beautiful country is part of that strip once known as Cherokee Strip or No Man's Land, the last area in the continental United States to be opened for homesteading. The history of the settled white man is scarcely more than a generation past in that section of the high plains.

My thanks to Truman and Fannie Tucker, Jennie Rose Benton, and M. T. and Ruby Easley, all of Kenton, Oklahoma, for sharing their own and their families' memories of the homesteading days in the Oklahoma panhandle out of which Old Ella's past is created. Very special thanks to my friends, Robert Carr and Ann Vincent, of Boise City, Oklahoma, for sharing themselves and their home and for worrying about rattlesnakes.

Finally, my appreciation to John H. Wright, D.V.M., of Hopkins, Minnesota, for a crash course in veterinary obstetrics. A person can never tell what information will be needed in the writing of a book.

M.D.B.